MY TOWN

WILLIAM WEGMAN

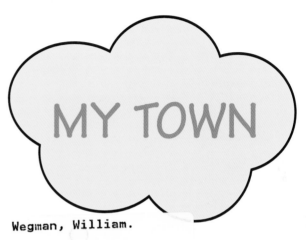

HYPERION

NEW YORK

Chip's homework is to hand in a report on a subject of his choosing. It's due tomorrow.

The library is a great place to get ideas.

COACH LOMBARDO

The coach always has good ideas. An inspiring pep talk is just what Chip needs.

What about talking to the
art teacher? She's creative.

Do *you* have any ideas for Chip?

School's out, maybe Chip should go to town.

POLICE OFFICER BADGERINO

Ideas come from everywhere. There is no one way. Look in all directions.

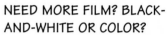

PHOTO STORE OWNER DOYLE

Speaking of late, Chip should get zipping on that report, or he'll never deliver it.

Will Fire Chief Chundo get Chip fired up, kindle his tinder, flame his passion, hose his hesitations?

The situation is really quite alarming. Chip's homework is due **tomorrow!**

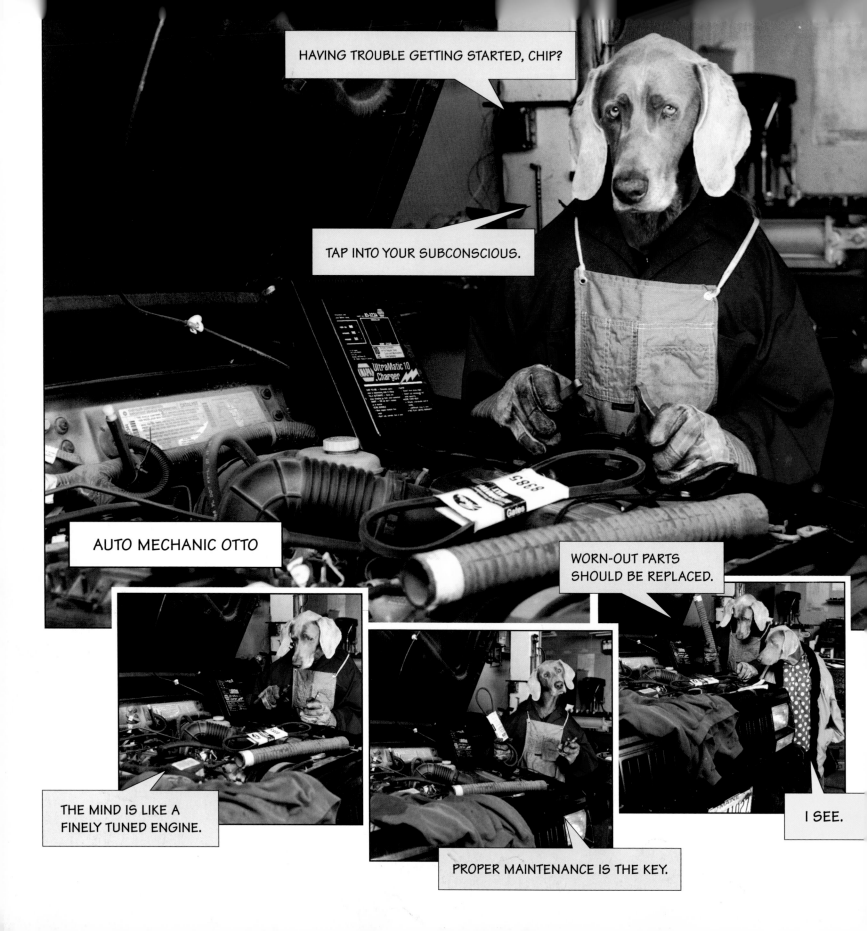

A visit to the auto repair shop and a quick check under the hood may help Chip.

ROTATE THE TIRES EVERY 5,000 MILES.

HMMM . . . RADIATOR HOSE OR FAN BELT?

HMMM . . .

KEEP THEM FILLED WITH AIR.

BUT DON'T OVERFILL THEM.

I'M UNDER TOO MUCH PRESSURE!

Perhaps getting his hair cut will make Chip
think better. Looking good is important.

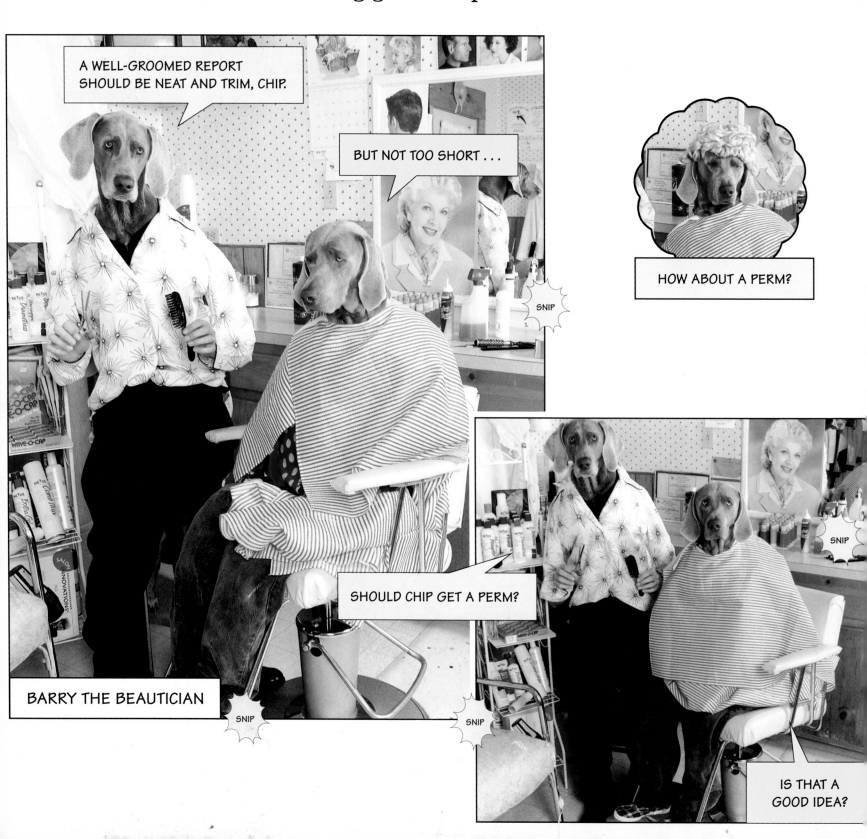

Chip should check out the supermarket and shop around for ideas.

Maybe Chip should see a doctor.

Is Chip okay?

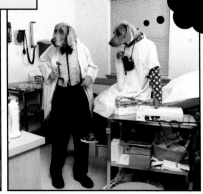

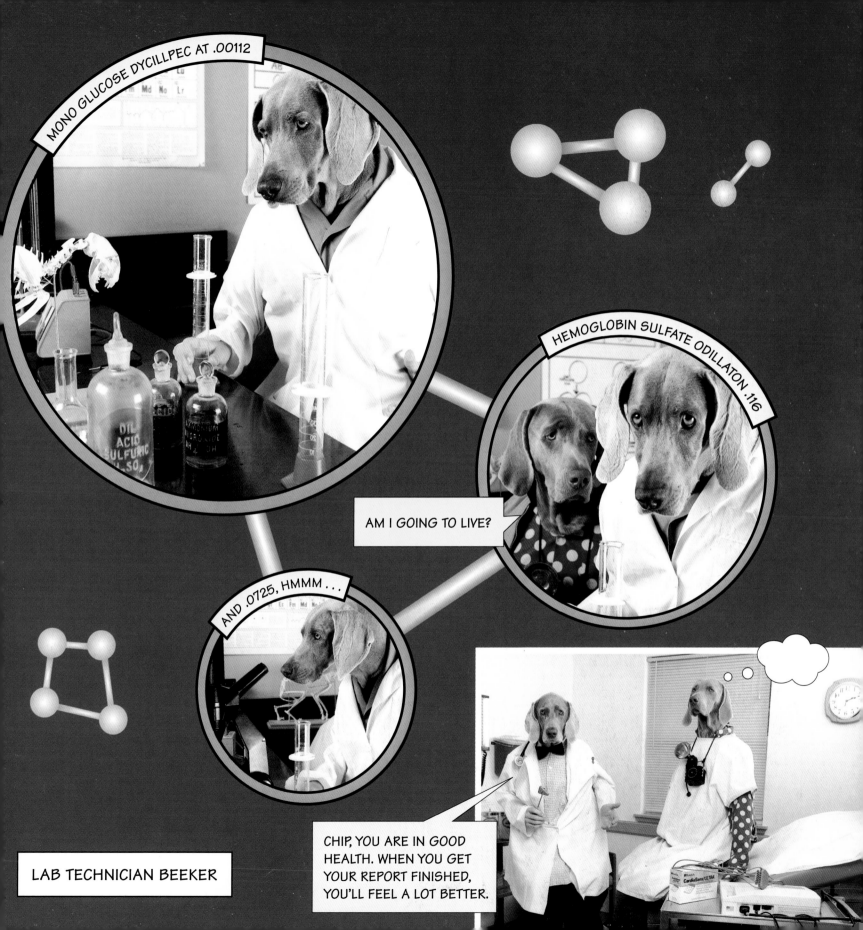

Chip is running out of time. Hey, wait a second . . .

Hey wait a second!

Teacher McMillan didn't say it had to be a *written* report (see page 3).

My Town

portraits
by Chip

A REPORT in pictures
a photo essay